Thoughtful Thinking

The Art of Poetry for Children

By Daksha Patel

Grosvenor House
Publishing Limited

This book is published by
Grosvenor House Publishing Ltd
Link House
140 The Broadway, Tolworth, Surrey, KT6 7HT.
www.grosvenorhousepublishing.co.uk

This book is a work of fiction. Any resemblance to
people or events, past or present, is purely coincidental.

A CIP record for this book
is available from the British Library

ISBN 978-1-80381-679-1

Dedication

I dedicate this book to my family
and Swami Vivekananda,
who is my role model.

This Book belongs to:

CONTENTS

ABOUT THE AUTHOR

Daksha Patel is of Indian origin. She was born in October 1975. She has a BA honours degree in English with History. She also has a postgraduate certificate in Primary Education that includes qualified teacher status from Brunel University.

Daksha is fluent in Gujarati and also holds a purple belt in the martial art of karate.

Daksha Patel's motto in life is that 'if at first you don't succeed in your aims and objectives then you should try, try and try again'. Education is for character-building too and it enables us to shine like stars when we succeed.

Other books by Daksha Patel (published by GHP) are:

Thoughtful Thinking: Short Stories for Children.
Thoughtful Thinking: Poems for Children.
Thoughtful Thinking: Haikus for Children.
Thoughtful Thinking: Book of Poetry for Children.
Thoughtful Thinking: Book of Haikus for Children.

HOW TO USE THIS BOOK

1. Read each poem carefully with the child or person about three times.

2. Try to remember the poems and say them out loud. Start with the haikus first.

3. Get the child or person to answer the comprehensions set in the book.

4. Colour in the pictures with accuracy to match with what the poem says. Use pencil colours to shade in with.

5. Use the glossary to test the child or person's knowledge of the special words. For example, you can ask the question: *What does alliteration mean?* And then check in the glossary for the answer.

ROBIN POEM

Of all the birds in the world,
The robin is the UK's favourite bird.

Arriving at Christmas-time,
When the weather is of snow,
The males and females look the same,
As they appear on Christmas cards for show.

With brown, white and orange feathers,
The robins stand up tall.
The robins eat worms, insects and seeds.

And, although the robins are still small,
They are highly territorial birds you see.
The robins line up along the branches of a tree.

They puff up their feathers till tall,
To keep their bodies warm inside.
Warm, from the cold wintery weather outside.

Also, the robins sing to each other.
They sing all year round.
And, they communicate to please each other,
With their melodious singing sounds.

ROBIN POEM COMPREHENSION

1. What bird is the UK's favourite?

2. What are the colours of the robin's feathers?

3. What do robins eat?

4. Do robins sing?

5. Why do robins puff up their feathers?

LADYBIRD POEM

Ladybird, ladybird,
You are the cutest of insects,
Because you are small.

Ladybird, ladybird,
You eat the aphids off our roses,
Before the petals fall.

Ladybird, ladybird,
The spots on you tell us your age,
Even though you are that small.

Ladybird, ladybird,
You can fly up high with your beetle wings,
Without coming to a fall.

Ladybird, ladybird,
Beauty can come with being that small.

Ladybird, ladybird,
You are the best insect of them all!

LADYBIRD POEM COMPREHENSION

1. What are aphids?

2. How can you tell the age of a ladybird?

3. Why is the ladybird cute?

4. Where can you find ladybirds?

5. What does a common ladybird look like?

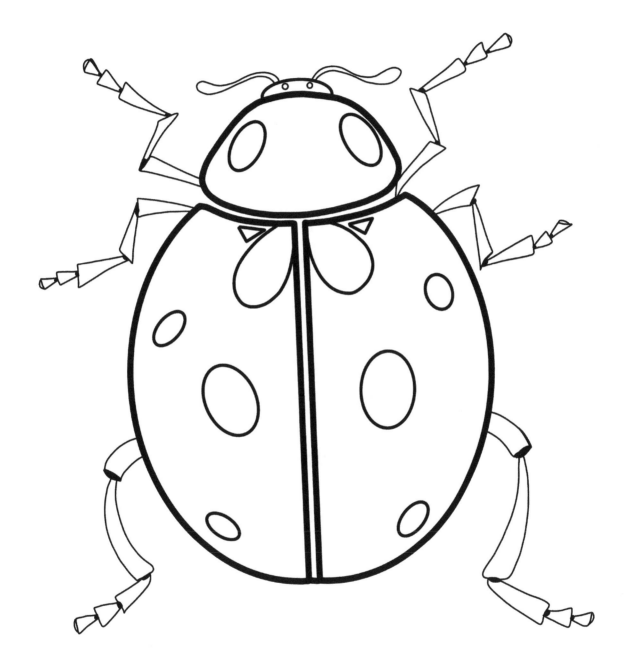

GOLDFISHES POEM

In a glass fishbowl,
As they swim in the clear water,

The goldfishes go around and around.

Opening and closing their mouths,
The fish see with open eyes,
Because they have no eyelids.

The goldfishes go around and around.

The goldfishes can survive in the coldest weather.
Outside, in the pond dug out of the ground,

The goldfishes go around and around.

But, the fishes are happiest and healthiest in mineral
water.
This gives them their clear sparkling eyes,
And their gold and orange bodies shimmer.
As they move and swim close to the fishbowl,

The goldfishes go around and around.

Also, when they eat their nutritious colourful worm flakes, really fast,
The goldfish swish their beautiful tails,
And swim past.
Without making a single sound,
They swim above the gravelled ground.

The goldfishes go around and around.

In the wild, the goldfishes would naturally stay together,
As if they were in a school of fish in the sea.
But, in their glass fishbowl,

The goldfishes go around and around.

COPY THE PICTURE

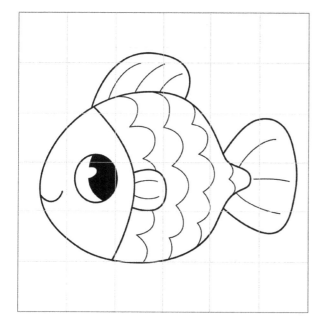

GOLDFISHES POEM COMPREHENSION

1. Do goldfishes have eyelids?

2. What does being in mineral water do for the goldfishes?

3. Can goldfishes survive in a cold pond, outside?

4. What food do the goldfishes eat?

5. What action do the goldfishes do all the time in the fishbowl?

BEES POEM

Like wearing black stripes on their yellow bodies with pride,

The bees all buzz around.

Collecting nectar from jumping from flower to flower,

The bees all buzz around.

As the yellow sticky pollen pollinates the colourful flowers outside,

The bees all buzz around.

When the honey is safe in the beehive trays, and dripping,

The bees all buzz around.

When humans take the honey from the beehive by smoking the bees out,

The bees all buzz around.

BEES POEM COMPREHENSION

1. Describe what the bees look like.

2. What do the bees collect from the flowers?

3. What food do bees make?

4. How do the humans get the bees out of the beehive?

5. What is the common action of the bees in the poem?

EAGLES POEM

Big and strong,
With a sharp beak,
The eagles are birds of prey.
Impressive hunters,
With large wingspans.
They are dark brown in colour.

The eagles fly, high in the sky.

Strong in vision,
They see everything on the ground.
With birds' eye vision,
They see like a map of the ground.
With sharp claws,
The eagles make a show of their power.

The eagles fly, high in the sky.

Because the eagle is America's national bird,
To the Native American Indians,
And to the modern Americans of today,
The eagle represents:
Strength, courage, freedom and power.

The eagles fly, high in the sky.

Also, as tradition tells us,
Eagle feathers are rewarded,
To Native American Indian warriors and chiefs,
For their acts of bravery and valour.
The Native American chief wears the feathers proudly in his headdress,
To show off his warrior skills,
And his tribal leadership position and power.

The eagles fly, high in the sky.

EAGLES POEM COMPREHENSION

1. What type of vision does the eagle have?

2. How can 'birds' eye vision' help us?

3. What is America's national bird?

4. Who wears eagle feathers in his headdress?

5. Do eagles eat meat?

HAIKU: ANT POEM

An army of ants,
Nesting in the big ant hill.
Thirsty for water.

HAIKU: ANTS POEM COMPREHENSION

1. What is an ant?

2. What type of poem is this?

3. Where is the ant nest?

4. Where is the alliteration in this poem?

5. Are the ants thirsty?

HAIKU: FAT POEM

Food is fun to eat,
A lot is not good for you.
Too much makes you fat.

HAIKU: FAT POEM COMPREHENSION

1. Is food fun to eat?

2. What type of poem is this?

3. Why is a lot of food not good for you?

4. In the poem, what do the first letters of each word read going downwards?

5. Is it good for your health to be fat?

HAIKU: JELEBI
(AN INDIAN SWEET) POEM

Like an orange web,
With a rose syrup through it.
A crispy, sweet taste.

Jalebi   Burfi   Sandesh   Gulab jamun

Peda   Kulfi   Gajar ka halwa   Kaju paan

Laddu   Shahi Tukda   Modak   Puran Poli

Indian desserts

HAIKU: JELEBI (AN INDIAN SWEET) POEM COMPREHENSION

1. What is the shape of the sweet compared to?

2. What type of poem is this?

3. What is the flavour of the syrup used?

4. What is the texture of the sweet like?

5. Have you ever eaten a jelebi?

THE ANSWERS TO THE COMPREHENSIONS

Robin poem

1. The robin.
2. Brown, white and orange.
3. Worms, insects and seeds.
4. Yes.
5. To keep their bodies warm inside.

Ladybird poem

1. Small flies.
2. You can count the spots on their back.
3. Because it is small.
4. In your garden or outside.
5. Red with black spots.

Goldfishes poem

1. No.
2. It gives the goldfishes clear sparkling eyes, bodies that shimmer and beautiful tails.
3. Yes.
4. Colourful worm flakes.
5. The goldfishes swim around and around.

Bees poem

1. They have black stripes on a yellow body with wings and a sting on their tail.
2. Nectar and sticky pollen.
3. Honey.
4. They smoke them out.
5. 'The bees all buzz around'.

Eagles poem

1. Strong vision and 'birds' eye vision'.
2. To make maps.
3. The eagle.
4. The Native American Indian Chief.
5. Yes.

Haiku: Ants poem

1. An insect.
2. A haiku and an acrostic poem.
3. In a hill.
4. In the first line: 'An army of ants'.
5. Yes.

Haiku: Food poem

1. Sometimes.
2. A haiku and an acrostic poem.
3. Because you can become fat.
4. FAT.
5. No.

Haiku: Jelebi (an Indian sweet) poem

1. A web.
2. A haiku.
3. Rose syrup.
4. Crispy and sticky.
5. Yes or no.

GLOSSARY

<u>Acrostic poem</u> - In this poem the first letter of each line spells a word. The word is the subject of the poem.

<u>Adjectives</u> are describing (descriptive) words such as striped, moving, furry.

<u>Adverbs</u> tell you how it's done, such as how someone eats, e.g., quickly.

<u>Alliteration</u> is the repeating of a sound, e.g., the snake slithered slowly.

<u>Haikus</u>: Short poems from Japan - they have three lines and 17 syllables in total.

<u>Metaphor</u> is when you compare something to something else without using 'like' or 'as'.

<u>Nouns</u> are naming words such as Daksha, Africa and door.

<u>Onomatopoeia</u> is a word used to make a sound, e.g., bang, click, hiss.

<u>Personification</u> is something that has a human quality attached to something like an object, e.g., the blackboard stares and the leaves smile.

<u>Prepositions</u> are where we, or something, is situated, e.g., we are *under* the bridge.

<u>Rhyme</u> is when the ending of the poem has the same sound as previous lines.

<u>Simile</u> is when you describe something similar to something else using the words 'like' or 'as'.

<u>Superlative</u> describes the highest degree of a quality (adjective or adverb), e.g., bravest, most beautiful.

<u>Verbs</u> are doing words, such as jump, dive, and sing.

<u>The difference between a verse and a stanza</u> is that verses are all equal and stanzas are chunks that are not equal.

BIBLIOGRAPHY/SOURCES

Internet Websites:

https://www.britannica.com.
https://the goldfishtank.com/goldfish-facts/.
https://www.google.com/Eagles, birds of prey.
https://www.rspb.org.ukRobin.
https://en.Wikipedia.org>wiki>Eagle.

Art Work Websites:

http://www.shutterstock.com

- Robin picture (in black & white).
- Ladybird picture (in black & white).
- Goldfish picture (in black & white).
- Copy goldfish picture (in black & white).
- Bees picture (in black & white).
- Eagle picture (in black & white).
- American Indians picture (in black & white).
- Ant and bugs picture (in black & white).
- Child eating picture (in black & white).
- Indian sweets picture (in black & white).
- Front cover picture of bees and hive (in colour).
- Back page picture of robin (in colour).

9 781803 816791